Nikki 1978

By Dorothy Hamilton
April, 1979

Linda's
Rain Tree

Linda's Rain Tree

Dorothy Hamilton
Illustrated by Ivan Moon

HERALD PRESS
Scottdale, Pennsylvania
Kitchener, Ontario
1975

Library of Congress Cataloging in Publication Data

Hamilton, Dorothy, 1906-
 Linda's rain tree.

 SUMMARY: Through a summer full of apprehensions
before she transfers to a new mostly white school, a
young black girl grows and blooms like her rain tree.
 [1. Family life — Fiction] I. Moon, Ivan. II. Ti-
tle.
PZ7.H18136Li   [Fic]   75-16301
ISBN 0-8361-1777-8
ISBN 0-8361-1778-6 pbk.

LINDA'S RAIN TREE

Copyright © 1975 by Herald Press, Scottdale, PA 15683
 Published simultaneously in Canada by Herald Press,
 Kitchener, ON N2G 1A7
Library of Congress Card Catalog Number: 75-16301
International Standard Book Number:
 0-8361-1777-8   (hardcover)
 0-8361-1778-6   (softcover)
Printed in the United States of America

To Derri

1

LINDA POWELL had been sitting on the back steps for half an hour or longer. She wasn't very comfortable because the board was splintered and rough. *But if I move down to the smooth place I can't see past the castor beans and the trash cans in the alley.*

She hadn't sat and stared at Gloria and the other girls. She just glanced that way once in a while, then looked down if she thought they were looking at her. They didn't need to think she wanted to go with them. She wouldn't even if they asked. She'd said "no" plenty of times.

Linda rested her chin on her doubled-up fist and thought about what was happening to these girls. *Just last year we were friends. Liked the same things mostly. Now all they got on their minds is parading up and down Eastside Avenue. That's why they're doing all that primping. Piling Gloria's hair up on top of her head and sprinkling sparkling stuff in Angelina's.*

The sun was warm for early June. Linda leaned back against the house and tilted her face upward. When she shut her eyes she could still see the golden light. She could hear cars whizzing along Eastside two blocks away. *I keep wondering why they call that street an avenue,* she thought. *It's not like the dictionary says — not lined with trees. There's not even any grass between the curb and the sidewalk.*

It's no wonder summertime doesn't seem so great, Linda thought. *Around here it's not like it is in books. Except in our yard and Mrs. Mozely's window box, there are no flowers. But the main thing wrong is that school's out.*

Linda loved school. That was another way she was different from the girls in Gloria's group. They hated school, at least that's what they said. Sometimes Linda thought they were just imitating Gloria. How'd she get to be the leader all at once? Who elected her as model? She was eight months older than the other girls. That was because she came up from Louisiana and hadn't started to school when she was six. But the age difference hadn't showed up until Gloria began to act like she was sixteen or older — several years beyond her age.

That's when Linda began to feel really left out. Up to then she'd decided when she'd rather read or take her little brothers to the park instead of playing house or skipping rope. *Now — well, I still decide — not to go strutting over on Eastside. But the difference is they're mad at me. Call me names.*

Linda began to feel that she'd been sitting on the back steps for an hour or more. She wiggled one foot to make the pins and needles feeling go away. *I know it's not late. Just a little past noon. The one o'clock whistle at the packing plant blew a few minutes ago.*

The girls were still over in Gloria's yard. But they acted like they were getting ready to leave. Linda could hear Aggie ask someone, "Are you *sure* this green vest looks all right?" Aggie was never sure about anything.

Linda slid down until she was halfway off the step and partly hidden behind the castor bean leaves. Her mother planted the big brown beans every spring, using two or three packages of seeds. She always said, "They make a lot of greenery and some shade, and give us a little privacy." None of their neighbors tried to make their yards look nice.

The Powells even had two trees. One was an apple tree with a crooked trunk. It had been there when they moved up from Indianapolis. It bore fruit some years but there were knots on one side of every apple. That's why Linda's brother Freddie called it the lopsided apple tree.

None of the Powells wanted anything to happen to the tree. The first thing after every thunderstorm someone looked to see if lightning had split the trunk. The boys could climb on the low limbs and pretend they were explorers or astronauts. Their mother sat in its shade while she sewed patches on jeans and mended clothes belonging to the ladies who paid her to do their ironings.

Even Linda's father was glad for the shade of the apple tree. He rested underneath it on sunny Sundays and on some afternoons before he went to work on the night shift at the wire factory.

Now he won't, Linda thought as she looked out over the yard. *He's away to some town looking for a job. Mama says it's hard telling if he'll find one or not. That we may have to make out till November when this layoff ends.*

She thought of leaving the step and swinging on the loop of rope which hung from the thickest limb of the apple tree. *Even if I am growing up I still like to swing. Maybe that's partly why Gloria and the others call me Baby Linda and ask if I'm scared to leave my playpen. They always say stuff like that when they see me swinging. And some other times.*

Thinking of trees reminded Linda that she'd forgotten to do one thing on her work chart. She'd made her bed, polished everyone's shoes for church the next day, and washed the breakfast dishes. She'd felt good when she put checks after these jobs. *I'll water my rain tree this afternoon when it's in the shade. Mrs. Julian's husband said not to water things when the sun is boiling down. It might cook them.*

Linda felt good whenever she looked at the little rain tree, even when it was black and bare in the wintertime. She felt loved and warm every time she remembered the day two years before when her teacher and her husband knocked at the front door. Linda's mother opened it a crack to see who was there. She didn't have any extra money for buying raffle tickets, or crepe paper flowers, or paying for subscriptions to magazines.

Linda peeked out of the window and saw Mrs. Julian. "It's the teacher," she whispered.

Mrs. Powell opened the door wider and said "Yes" when the teacher asked, "Is Linda here? Oh, hello there. We brought you something."

Linda looked at her mother's face and thought, *She's puzzled too.*

"This is my husband," Mrs. Julian said. "He's the gardener in our family. I brought him along to set out Linda's rain tree. If that's all right."

"Well, yes," Mrs. Powell said. "But I don't understand. "Why — "

Mrs. Julian smiled. Linda could see her eyes shining behind her glasses. "I'll tell you if you'll tell us where you'd like to have the tree planted out here."

"No, no," Linda's mother said. "It couldn't live here. Almost no one respects anyone's property. But we have a good fence around the back."

They'd decided the tree should be in the sun and away from the fence. As Mr. Julian spaded a hole Linda and the women talked, hugging close to the house to keep out of the chill wind.

At first they said polite things like "I'm sorry if we're bothering you" and "It was real nice of you to come."

Then the teacher said, "I'm a creature of impulse — at times, at least. The idea of getting a rain tree for Linda came to me the day we took her class to Memorial Park at New Castle. The other children ran and squealed all the way down the circular slide, and played on the monkey bars. But this child of yours was more interested in the trees and bushes. And when we came to the rain trees her eyes sparkled. She said, 'The flowers fall like rain in golden sprays.' "

Mrs. Julian explained that the nursery was having a two-for-the-price-of-one sale. "And we don't have toom for two more trees — hardly enough for one. So! Here we are."

As Linda thought back to that day she realized that the teacher was trying to make her feel comfortable about taking the gift. *She never wanted to hurt anybody's pride.*

2

LINDA decided she'd swing awhile even if the girls hadn't left Gloria's yard. *I don't have to let them keep me from doing what I like. Just like they can't make me go with them.*

Not all the leaves had opened on the apple tree. Spring had been late coming to Indiana and a late frost had slowed down the appearance of green on the branches. As Linda shoved herself into a swaying arc she could see patches of silvery blue sky. She pushed until her toes touched the outer twigs on the lower limbs. The knotted rope squeaked with her weight. Then she let the swing slow down, slower — and slower — *Let the old cat die*, she thought.

When her feet touched the dust in the hollowed-out place, she twisted around and around letting the rope unwind. She liked this feeling of being moved by some unseen force. She felt in place and upheld.

But Linda knew that many kinds of power operated in her life. Some of them made her uneasy or sad, and most of all scared. Mainly because she didn't know what or where they were. Aunt Claudia, who was the oldest member of Bethel Church, said the devil was fighting for control of the world.

A lot of children worried about what Aunt Claudia told their Sunday school class. They were glad she didn't take Miss Cora's place very often. Some even slipped out of church when Aunt Claudia started toward the pew in the back corner. They had plenty of time to get away. The substitute teacher stopped to shake hands with people on both sides of the aisle. Linda's father said Aunt Claudia acted "biggety," like she was the preacher.

Linda didn't like thinking about the devil. She felt fidgety when someone said that Satan was getting ahold of anyone, like he was grabbing them from around a corner or in a dark alley.

I wonder what Mama thinks about the devil, Linda thought as she rested one cheek against the rope. *I'll ask her someday when she's not so tired.*

An airplane droned overhead and a radio blared from the house next door. These added noises muffled the sound of the girls' voices. Linda caught a glimpse of purple and raised up to see the group go out of sight. She knew all of them — Gloria, Leeora, Aggie, and the Bain sisters. They were always

Before Linda scooted out of the swing she heard someone say, "Hi, Linda."

together. But not Corey Williams. *What's she doing tagging along? She's too young for them.*

No one in the group paid any attention to Linda. *They didn't even look my way. That suits me just fine!* But she couldn't help feeling left out — alone. She wished she'd gone over to the park with her brothers even if all they wanted to do was play on the jungle gym and swing on the maypoles

I could go to the library, she thought. *And maybe help Mrs. Ferguson read to the tots or something.*

Linda was a good reader. Her mother had taught the Powell children to take care of books. She often said, "No teacher has ever had to send a note home saying my young ones messed up a book."

Linda's mother couldn't read well enough to enjoy it. Figuring out the words was hard work. That's one reason why she was so proud of Linda. "That girl of ours, she knows her sounds and can figure out words with as many as twelve letters in them." Lots of times she begged, "Read to me, honey, while I work on this mountain of clothes. Seems like this old iron runs smoother if my mind's not on every wrinkle."

Before Linda scooted out of the swing she heard someone say, "Hi, Linda." Corey was coming around the corner of the yard.

"I just saw you with Gloria's crowd," Linda said.

"I know," Corey said. "They asked me to go for a walk with them. I backed out."

"Good thing," Linda said.

"What makes you say that?" Corey asked. "Don't you like Gloria and Aggie anymore?"

"Oh, I guess," Linda said. "Why don't we go over

20

and sit in the shade. 'Less you're scared of getting · green stains on your skirt."

"No matter," Corey said. "It's from a rummage sale."

"It's pretty anyway," Linda said. "And I suppose your mama could wash out grass stains. Mine does."

"Not mine," Corey said. "She don't hardly ever wash — just goes back to another sale."

Linda felt sorrier for Corey than she ever had before. She never did look happy. *But a lot of kids don't.* She remembered times when Corey didn't have any lunch and pretended she wasn't hungry. That was back before free lunches started. And when Scooter Williams first ran away and left his family, Corey had cried a lot at school. "He treated us real bad most of the time," Corey said once. "But he's still my daddy."

Now she looks — lost, Linda thought. *Like she doesn't belong anywhere.*

"You don't sound like you're sure," Corey said. "About what?"

"About liking Gloria and Aggie and the others."

"I used to," Linda said. "Especially Angelina. But — well, she's different. Or maybe it's me."

"No, I don't think so," Corey said. "You seem the same. 'Course I never did know them too well. They never paid no mind to me. 'Cepting to call me Baggie."

"Why did they call you a thing like that?"

"'Cause. They said my clothes came from other folks' rag bags. Which is true."

"Some of mine do," Linda said. "My mama says

pride that makes folks not use good stuff is wasteful."

Corey leaned over and watched ants scurry up and down a little hill of fine dirt. "Busy little fellers, where you going?"

"They're working," Linda said.

"Doing what?"

"Building an anthill."

"For what?"

"I don't really know," Linda said. "I'll have to look it up at the library."

"Why?" Corey asked.

"So I'll know," Linda said. "I like to find out about things — about life."

Neither girl said anything for a while. A garbage truck jolted down the alley and a baby cried from the second story in the house across the alley.

"That's what Gloria said when she was coaxing me to go walking over on Eastside. So I could learn about life. Do you know what she meant?"

"I'm afraid so. A little anyhow. And I don't want to know any more. And don't you dare go with them. If you know what's good for you, you'll say 'no' next time."

"I keep wondering why they wanted me," Corey said. "I mean all those girls have such neat clothes. Did you see Aggie's vest! All those silky tassels."

"I saw."

"I don't understand something else," Corey said. "What's it to you where I go? You act like it makes a difference. Like you care or something."

"Well, I do. Someone always does. Don't you know they do?"

"No, I never heard of that before."

3

LINDA tried to think of something she and Corey could do together. *Something which would be fun for both of us. She doesn't like to read. So she wouldn't want to go to the library. And I don't want to go to the park. It's about as bad as Eastside Avenue. Older boys driving around in cars all the time. Stopping girls.*

"What would you like to do?" Linda asked.

"What's *to* do around here?" Corey said.

"Well, a lot really," Linda said. "I read. And Mama's teaching me how to knit. I help her fold clothes and deliver ironings. Besides that, I go to the

Y for swimming lessons. Would you like to go?"

"I don't think so," Corey said. "It's a lot of bother catching a bus and everything."

"It's still fun," Linda said.

"Why does your mother do other folks' ironing?" Corey asked. "My mom says she's foolish. To be slaving for uptown folks."

Linda's face felt hot. She didn't like thinking that other people talked bad about her mama.

"She does it to earn money. To buy us things — like my new boots and curtains for our windows."

"She could get a lot without bothering. From Welfare and places like that."

Linda almost bit her tongue, trying to keep from saying that the Powells didn't take handouts. *But no use hurting Corey's feelings. If she doesn't see anything wrong with the way they live, I don't need to make her ashamed.*

Corey stretched and yawned. "I might as well go home and take a nap. If it's not too noisy."

Linda was relieved but she hid her feelings. After Corey crossed the alley, Linda went into the house. It was dark until her eyes adjusted to coming in from the bright sunshine. She heard the hissing and the thumps of her mother's steam iron coming from the front of the house.

"Why're you ironing in the living room, Mama?"

"'Cause there's a puff of breeze coming through the door once in a while. That's why. I began to wonder what had happened to you?"

"I've been talking to Corey. She started to go with Gloria's group, then came back."

"They ask you to tag along?"

26

"No," Linda said. "It would have been a waste of breath." She sat down on the floor near the open door and pulled up her legs so she could hug her knees.

"Mama. Why are some kids in a hurry to grow up.?"

Mrs. Powell turned to put a white shirt on a hanger before she answered. "I reckon it's kind of natural. And you can hardly blame them for wanting to get away from this part of the city. But they don't have any idea of what they're rushing into."

"I don't think this place is so bad," Linda said. "I'm in no hurry to get away."

"Honey. That's the nicest thing your mama could hear."

"Why. What's so nice?"

"Well — I strain and ache to keep you and your brothers safe and protected. To make home a nice place. No matter if we do live in a run-down part of town. Could be I'm getting it done?"

"You going to deliver that ironing?" Linda asked.

"Not this one — it's Mrs. Ramsey's. She always comes. Says it's easier for her than it would be for me to lug it over on the bus."

"Is it all right if I go to the library?" Linda asked. "Or should I watch the boys?"

"They're being watched. That young fellow from the Neighborhood Center took them for a walk. He called it a hike."

"Mr. Haines."

"You know him?"

"Sure. He's a teacher. Not mine. In a second-grade room."

27

"Does he get paid for taking boys for a walk? Is this a summer job?"

"I don't know," Linda said. "Well, I might as well go. Any special books you want me to bring back?"

"Maybe this is a sign I'm getting on, but I like those old-time stories, you know — by the lady who writes a lot of them."

"Laura Ingalls Wilder," Linda said. "I like them too." She didn't tell her mother that she'd read every one in the series. *If Mama wants to hear them I'd read them all again — I might anyway. Some books are that special.*

Linda didn't have to walk along Eastside Avenue to get to the library. She crossed it at the Wolf Street corner and cut through the alley to the new cement block building.

I'm sure glad they put a branch out here, she thought as she walked through the narrow entrance. *I'd not get to go uptown whenever I took a notion.*

One of the library aides was reading to a small group of young children — only four of them. Linda tiptoed to the stacks to the young teens section. She liked to read stories about kids who were a little older — but not too old. First she ran her finger along the rows, looking for books which were new. She pulled out five and sat down on the two-step ladder to see what was written on the cover.

She decided one book wasn't for her. She didn't know why. *Maybe because it's about rich kids.* She was about to put it back. *But that's not fair. Like Mama says, you can't always tell a book by its cover and besides maybe these kids have problems too. Or are nice.*

28

She started to gather up the five books when she remembered the ones her mama wanted. She was sliding the ladder along the aisle when she heard some sniffling sounds. At first she thought that whoever was between the next two rows of shelves had a cold. Then she heard choking sobs.

Linda stood still, not knowing which way to go. *Maybe whoever's over there wouldn't want me to see her. Sometimes I'm that way when I'm sad. It's like a loneliness — the kind other people can't help.* She stepped to the end of the stacks and started to the desk to have her books stamped.

Something made her turn back and walk to the next row of shelves. *I'm curious. I can't stand not to know who's crying.* She was surprised to see a tall girl with long silvery and gold hair leaning against the back wall. *That's the new library aide. What did Mrs. Ferguson say her name was — something like Amy — but that's not it.*

I guess I'd better not say anything to her. She'd probably not want to hear anything I could think of. What could a girl my age say to help a senior, especially a white girl?"

4

AS LINDA turned, a book slipped from the crook
of her arm. She tried to catch it, but it thumped
against the end of the shelves, then clumped to the
floor. The library aide turned and said, "Hello. I
didn't know anyone was near."

"I'm ready to go. Well, that's not true. I wanted
some Wilder books. They're in this last section. But I
didn't want to bother you."

"That's all right. After all, libraries are places
where people come to borrow books. They're not
built for walls to cry on." She hooked her long
hair behind her ears and dabbed her reddened nose

with a wadded tissue.

Linda opened the drawstring bag her mother had crocheted and said, "Here, that Kleenex looks pretty soggy."

"I know," the tall girl said. "Thank you. What's your name? I've seen you but you were always lost in a book."

"I'm Linda Powell."

"And I'm Amory Clark."

"That's a pretty name. I never heard it before."

"My mother named me — from a book." Then Amory's eyes filled up again. She shook her head so hard that her hair flipped and whipped across her face. "There I go again. I probably shouldn't have come to work so soon after."

Linda didn't say anything. But that didn't mean that questions weren't jumping around in her mind. *So soon after what? What kind of problems bothered girls with smooth clothes like Amory's cream-colored suede suit and soft brown calf high boots? Girls who could get good jobs as library aides?*

"Do you have time to talk, Linda?" Amory asked.

"Sure. If you want."

"I do. I'll tell you what! You get your books, then tell Mrs. Ferguson I'm going to take my break now. And I'll go to the washroom and try to get rid of some of the puffiness and redness. Meet me on the stone bench under the tree."

Linda checked out her books and gave the librarian Amory's message. Her feelings were a little mixed up as she waited on the cool bench. *Why does she want to talk to me? Is it because I'm the one who saw her crying? Looks like she'd want to*

*Amory jabbed the straw up and down in the cup so
hard the pale amber drops splashed into the air.*

tell her troubles to someone she knows. Or is this something she doesn't want them to know?

Amory came out, walking slowly, carrying two paper cups. "Here's some cream soda," she said. "I don't know what you like," she said. "But at least this is cold and wet."

"This is fine, thank you."

Amory sat down but she didn't say anything for what seemed a long time. Linda began to think she'd changed her mind about wanting to talk to her — or to anyone.

"It's really rough," Amory said after she'd sipped more than half of the cooling drink. She jabbed the red and white straw up and down in the cup so hard that pale amber drops splashed into the air. "I know it happens. To some of my friends. One parent or another does it. But I never thought it of mine. Of either of them. Especially not of my father."

What is she talking about? Linda thought, *Is her father wanting a divorce? Or is he on drugs? Or does he drink a lot?*

Amory pounded the stone bench with one doubled-up fist.

It's a wonder her hand doesn't bleed, Linda thought.

"But I should have seen," Amory said. "I mean there were signs. Like longer trips — he *said* on business. And not much talking at the table. But I just thought it was because both of them were busy — had a lot on their minds. Mother with civic theater and clubs. Dad was making the business go. Now — he's what's gone."

36

"You mean — he left. That's what's bothering you?"

"That's right. With no warning. Not even a note on the hall table, like in books. Just a telegram which came today — a three-word message — "Won't be back.""

"Maybe he'll change his mind," Linda said.

"Mother doesn't think so. *She's* not wasting any time about making sure he won't. She's seeing a lawyer — right this minute."

"Did you — do you feel close to your father?"

Amory nodded. "That's what hurts the worst. He didn't say anything to me — wait a minute! Perhaps he tried. When he talked about my birthday. It's three days from now. I remember exactly what he said. 'Your gift will come by mail this time. With a special message. Don't be angry with me until you read it!' At the time I just thought he was planning to be on another business trip. Now I see what he meant."

A boy rode past on a bicycle with a tin can trailing at the end of a piece of string. "Now why does he want to make so much clatter?" Amory said.

"Probably because he saw someone else do the same thing," Linda said.

"Are you shocked?" Amory asked. "Because my father deserted us?"

"No," Linda said. "This happens a lot around here. But I guess I am sort of surprised. I mean, I didn't know rich kids had the same problems."

"You think I'm rich?"

"Well, your clothes are beautiful and once I saw you come in a neat car."

"That's mine," Amory said. "I do have a lot of things. No problems about money. Just problems."

Linda thought of her mother, how she worked for hours every day to earn money to pay bills. And she compared the trips her father took to hunt a job with the way Mr. Clark had left. *Papa never wants to go. He keeps telling us that over and over. And he comes back whenever Mama hears that any plants or places are taking on workers.*

Amory looked at her watch. "It's time for me to get back to work. I wouldn't want to lose this job. Not now. I'd rather be here than at home with Mother's bitterness."

Linda surprised herself by asking, "Why do you want to work?"

Amory tilted her head back so that the light shining through the leaves made patches on her face. Some were bright, some were shadows. "That's an easy question to answer. I *love* books. Always have. I've worked in the school library since I was a freshman. And I've had it with loafing during the summer. Swimming and tennis are all right. But enough's enough."

She stood up, then leaned over and ran one finger down Linda's cheek. "Do you know something! You're a sweetheart to listen to me. I hope we see more of each other."

"So do I," Linda said.

As Linda walked home she felt both happy and sad. *I'm lucky that my parents think it's so important to keep our home a safe place. And I'm sad for Amory.*

She was in a hurry to tell her mother about meeting Amory. *Will she be surprised that Amory would talk to me about her unhappiness? Will she think it strange that someone who's a senior and has her very own car felt free about talking to little old me?*

Linda had noticed that her mother was a little shy around white people. She didn't even say much to Mrs. Ramsey who came almost every week. *I know Mama likes her and appreciates getting the ironings to do. She's always saying that Mrs. Ramsey pays extra money for good work.*

She remembered the day the teacher and her husband had brought the rain tree Mama was polite but seemed uneasy. Is it because Mama didn't graduate from school? Linda knew a lot of mothers, most of them really, wouldn't go to school even when teachers wrote notes. *It's as if people are divided up in sections like the knives and forks and spoons in our silverware drawer. Only I'm always jumping in and talking to someone from other places — like Amory.*

5

THE SUN was hidden by smoky clouds before Linda checked out her books and left the library. The wind came in puffs and blew crumpled paper cups and wadded candy wrappers along the sidewalk. The cups bumped and the waxed papers rustled.

It's going to rain, Linda thought. *Maybe storm. I'd better hurry.* It was so dark by the time she reached Eastside Avenue that some of the cars had already turned on their headlights. Lightning slashed across the sky and Linda could hear thunder rolling above the roar of traffic.

Linda's mother was standing at the door. "My lands,

43

honey, I was getting worried about you."

"Well, I was getting a little worried about me too," Linda said. "Do you think it's going to be a bad storm?"

"Hard to say," her mother said. "When it's been hot like this for a spell bad weather sometimes follows."

"Are the boys home?"

"Yes indeedy. They came scooting in the back door a jiffy after they heard the first clap of thunder. They're upstairs. Either on their bed or under it. They were trying to decide which was safer as they scrambled up the steps."

The wind was so strong that Linda and her mother had to shut both doors and all the windows except those on the west. For a while the house was as hot as a bake oven. Within fifteen minutes the storm and shower were over. The rain had cooled the air and washed away much of the dust and soot. Linda thought of her little rain tree and hurried to the back door.

"Oh, my goodness. It's leaning way down. Almost touching the ground."

"Mama, come look. Is my tree ruined for good and ever?"

Mrs. Powell walked out to the back step. "No, honey. It's been blown by the wind. But it'll straighten itself up in no time at all. It'll be all right in a jiffy."

"How can it?" Linda asks. "What makes things get all right all by themselves?"

"Not *what*, Linda Amelia. Who? The Lord above has laws for such as that."

"For people too?"

"Yes. For people. Only trouble is people got the right to choose if they go along with Him. And they don't always obey."

Linda thought of Amory and her sadness. Who was deciding to make things bad for her? Was it her mother or father or maybe both?"

"I'd better scratch around and fix some supper for my little chicks," Linda's mother said. "What sounds good?"

"Oh, strawberry shortcake or pepperoni pizza or hot dogs."

"That's some combination. The hot dogs we can manage. Mrs. Ramsey paid me for doing her ironing. You want to scoot over to the Jiffy Market."

"Why not the big store? You say it's cheaper."

"Now you know why. There's no way you can keep from passing that hangout — what's it called?"

"The Zebra Cage."

"I don't aim to send you over that way. I don't like to pass there myself — 'less there's someone along."

Linda understood. She'd heard a lot of whisperings about what went on in that eating place. About what was sold besides malts and hamburgers and ice-cream floats. She wouldn't have passed it on her way to the supermarket. Her mother didn't need to tell her to stay away. It meant walking four extra blocks. She'd done it lots of times without saying anything. She figured it wasn't any use to cause any more worry, especially if the tales about drugs and things might not all be true.

The sun came out from behind the rain-misted clouds as Linda returned home with the pound of meat and package of buns. The golden light of the sun seemed to tint the green grass a shade of brass. And the leaves of the rain tree were glossy and shining.

Linda's brothers had heard her voice as she came home through the alley. They wore faded swimming trunks. Freddie was standing on an overturned garbage can beneath a limb of the lopsided apple tree. He held on to a stout twig and shook hard back and forth. Showers of raindrops glistened on both boys' faces and shoulders.

"Does Mama know what you're doing?"

"She knows," Leo said. "She tell us this is the only kind of shower bath us Powells have."

Linda's mother was washing leaf lettuce from the garden patch. That's another way the Powells were different. They heard about the plots of city land on the other side of the school and claimed a square for raising vegetables. It wasn't easy hoeing and planting and picking — and sometimes it was discouraging, like when some kids got the crazy idea that it was fun to mash down plants or steal vegetables. But it did help stretch their grocery money.

"Want me to do that?" Linda asked.

"I don't care if you do. I'll get these hot dogs under the top oven burner and spoon some peach slices on cottage cheese."

"I been wanting to tell you something, Mama," Linda said as she dipped crinkly leaves up and down in the cold water. "I got to talking to a girl over at the library. She was real sad. That's what started us talking — when I walked around the stacks and found her leaning against the wall and crying."

Linda told her mother why Amory was unhappy

and that they'd gone outside and talked a long time. "It seemed to help her to be able to tell someone how she truly felt."

"It does lots of times," Mrs. Powell said. " 'Course, a person has to be careful who they pick for unloading troubles. Was this girl from around here?"

"Oh, no. She's real rich. Lives over in Kimberly Acres. That's close to the college. I guess I never thought that anyone like Amory had problems the same as people here do."

"Honey," Mrs. Powell said, "problems don't come in colors. People do, but not problems."

As Linda blotted the moisture from the lettuce with a bleached flour sack, a question took shape in her mind. *Do girls like Amory and her friends parade up and down the streets? Do such things go on over there where avenues are really avenues?*

She wanted to ask her mother the question that was on her mind but her brothers came in the door.

"You boys are dripping wet," their mother said.

"I know," Freddie said. "But we can't get any wetter. We've used up all the raindrops. Now we're hungry."

They were eating when Mrs. Mozely came to the back door. "Miss Powell," she said, "the wire mill foreman called. Says to tell you the furnaces are being fired and your man can start work Monday."

"Oh that's good news," Mrs. Powell said. "Why don't you come in and eat a bite with us?"

"Well, since you insist," the neighbor said. "A body don't have much taste eatin' alone like I do."

"Just set yourself down," Mrs. Powell said. "Linda will get you tableware. I'm going to dash right down to the phone booth and put in a call to Joseph. It's a good thing Mrs. Ramsey paid me partly in coins. Now you stay, Mrs. Mozely! We'll visit a while. Then maybe sit out in the yard and enjoy the cool of the evening together."

6

LINDA felt safe and full of hope as she drifted into
sleep that night. The rain had cooled the air and she
didn't have to lie with her head at the foot of the bed
to be comfortable. She liked what she saw from the
open window but not what she heard.

The sky was clear, decorated with golden stars and
a silvery moon. But the street noises were loud and
sometimes frightening. People screamed, sirens wailed,
and tires screeched. Nighttime wasn't a time of rest
over on Eastside.

Mrs. Mozely had stayed until after nine-thirty.
She wasn't ready to leave when the rain-cooled air

51

drove them inside. She told tales about how it was to grow up in Louisiana where her folks worked in the rice fields. She remembered how excited her parents were about coming up North when her uncle Rafe had been up here a year or so. "He wrote a card saying Pap could get a job at the wire mill. We scraped up every penny. Mama sold her chickens and our little dab of furniture. Our old car nearly gave out when he crossed the Ohio River. We barely made it the rest of the way."

"Did you ever go back?" Linda asked. "Back to Louisiana, I mean."

"Not in body. Only in my mind's eye," Mrs. Mozely said. "Seems like the longer I was up here, the better life down there looked."

"It's that way, I guess," Mrs. Powell said. "My mama told me her memory of Alabama was brightest when snow came a drifting over Indiana, and when times was the hardest."

Linda's brothers were both asleep — one at one end of the couch, one at the other — before the neighbor went home. "I should've marched them right up to bed when their eyelids began to get heavy," Mrs. Powell said. "Now they'll be stiff-legged and weigh twice as much as usual."

"I'll help you, Mama," Linda said. "But I'm not one bit sleepy."

"Come to think of it, neither am I. Something special on your mind?"

"Well, yes. I wanted to ask something when Mrs. Mozely was talking. But you'd probably say it was not polite to interrupt."

"Ask what?"

"Why did so many people come up North? I mean things aren't so great for everyone here."

"No. No, they's not. But they be some better." Linda's mother leaned over and unlaced her canvas shoes. She took a deep breath, as she curled and uncurled her toes and rested her head on the high back of the wooden rocker.

"But as bad as it seems, where they come from is worse. Some leastways. Maybe there's not a lot of difference but enough to keep them here."

"Did you ever think of going back to Alabama?"

"No. That's 'cause I never lived there. And only visited a time or two. This is home for me."

"For me too," Linda said.

" 'Course I don't have my feet glued to this street or my rocking chair nailed to this floor boards. I could stand to live where it's quieter and cleaner. Once your papa gets a year's steady work we might just make it."

"To where, Mama? Where could we live?"

"Well, that's the problem," her mother said. "There's places we can't buy or rent."

Linda knew what her mother meant. She didn't understand why they couldn't move to any street in town. She just knew they couldn't.

For some reason Linda thought of the little rain tree. It could grow in all kinds of places like parks and in Mrs. Julian's yard and maybe on her side of Eastside Avenue. This thought led to another. "Mama," she said. "I forgot to water my little tree."

"Well, no matter — this time. The good Lord took care of that for you."

Linda was too sleepy to look out the window or even

53

listen for the noises of the night by the time she climbed the steep stairs. She didn't know what was going on in the outside world until she heard a pounding on the front door. At first she thought it was part of a dream.

She tiptoed to the window. She couldn't see who was on the porch but she could hear her mother's voice and someone crying.

I don't know if I want to go down or not. Something scary has probably happened. She felt like jumping back in bed and pulling the covers over her head. But she walked to the stairway and listened until she recognized Corey's voice.

"Oh, Miss Powell, I just know a terrible thing is about to happen to Gloria. You should've heard her."

"Heard her what?" Linda's mother asked.

"Yelling. Like she was being choked or something. But I reckon she wasn't. No one could make that much noise if someone was grabbing at their throat."

Linda went downstairs but her bare feet didn't make enough noise to let her mother know she was near enough to hear. "Try to keep your voice low," Mrs. Powell said. "No need to scare Linda."

"I'm already scared, Mama."

"Oh, honey. I'm sorry I didn't shut the stairway door."

"That wouldn't have helped. I heard the pounding."

Linda's mother went to the kitchen and came back with a glass of milk for both girls. Between sips Corey told what she knew. She was alone in the house and had fallen asleep on the day bed while she was watching TV. "My uncle's back and that always means I get scooted out of my own bed."

At first she thought the screaming was part of the show. But whoever was yelling kept right on during the commercial so she looked out the window and saw Gloria on the sidewalk with this boy — or man. He was pulling her toward the car and she was screaming and trying to jerk away.

"Where's Gloria now?" Mrs. Powell asked.

"At home, I guess. The car tore off when another came down the street."

"You didn't go over to see if Gloria's all right?"

"No, ma'am. I saw her pop come out and yank her into the house. That's when I came over here."

"But I don't understand. If you think Gloria's okay — " Linda said. Then she stopped. "Maybe I do. You came because you're scared."

"That's right," Corey said. "Fear's sort of creepy. I couldn't stand being alone."

"Then you stay right here. You can sleep on the couch," Linda's mother said. "And I'll wait up till I think your folks are back. So they won't be a fretting!"

"But it's awful late, Mrs. Powell. And they may be a lot later."

"I'll wait," Linda's mother said. "I can do some cat-napping here in this chair. Linda, you bring down an extra blanket for Corey. The night's turned real cool all of a sudden."

Linda couldn't get to sleep for a while. She wasn't really worried about Gloria. She had some idea of what had happened. "Some of those guys she flirts around with over on Eastside probably came back at night, thinking that's what Gloria wanted. Or maybe they were drunk or drugged, not knowing what they were doing.

Linda wished she didn't know about such things. But there was no way to keep from knowing. She tried. She walked away from girls who gathered in little clusters in the rest rooms and halls and on the playground. Sometimes they called her goody-goody. But she figured she had a right to decide what went in her ears.

Linda wished she had a big eraser that would wipe all the bad things out of the world. But she'd decided it was up to each person to do that. Even if it wasn't easy she would keep on trying.

7

COREY was gone when Linda went downstairs the next morning. The house was quiet. Usually she could tell what her mother was doing by listening. But now there was no thumping of the iron, no clinking of silverware, or whisking of the broom.

She tiptoed across the kitchen and looked into the downstairs bedroom. "Come in, Linda Amelia," her mother said.

"You sick?"

"Now when do that ever happen to your mama?"

"Well, not often. But it could."

"I s'pose. But this is not the time," Mrs. Powell

said. "Come curl up beside me and we'll plan the day ahead."

"Does it need to be planned?" Linda asked. "I thought what had to be done was unrolled like a rug."

"Most times, yes. But I'm caught up on my work. And your paper will be rolling in tomorrow, early. So I figured we'd do something happy-like getting ready."

"That's why you're still in bed?" Linda said. "Figuring what to do?"

"Not exactly. I just woke up when I heard you pit-patting down the steps. Corey's folks didn't get home until way after midnight."

"Did she go home then?"

"Yes. I told her she could sleep on. But she'd been tossing and turning and making moaning noises. Then she heard me go call to her mama. So I walked her across the alley."

"Her folks didn't even come get her."

"No. I couldn't tell if they rightly understood what I said. And I sure couldn't make out what they were a-saying. Mostly mumbles."

Linda sat up and peered out the small square window. "Looks like the sun might be shining out there," she said.

"Let's get up and go out," Mrs. Powell said. "I always did like the look of things after a rain — clean and sort of new. A real pretty sight."

The grassy spots in the yard glistened with early morning dew. It was as if sparkly jewels had been sprinkled on a dark green rug. "Seems like these castor beans have grown overnight," Mrs. Powell said.

60

"*Do you think my little tree will bloom this year?*"
Linda asked.

"This one's about as high as the windowsill already."

Linda walked across the wet grass to the rain tree. Its sprays of leaves glistened in the silvery sunlight. "Mama," she called. "Do you think my little tree will bloom this year?"

"If I had a dime for every time you asked that question we'd be a sight richer. It's too early to tell. Blooming time's not the same for all living things. What did the teacher's man say?"

"I knew that it wouldn't have flowers the first summer 'cause moving it was a shock. But this is the second year."

"But it's still early summer. Real early. So give it time."

During breakfast the Powells talked about what they'd do to get ready for Father's homecoming.

"I'll give the house a once-over polish. Then we'll go to the supermarket."

"Uptown, Mama?" Freddie asked.

"No. I'm thinking we'll go to the one in the new shopping center. We have to change buses and lug our groceries a far piece. But they's things over there we've not laid our eyes on for a long time."

She told the boys to pick up fallen twigs and leaves blown down in the storm and put them in the trash barrel in the alley. "Time we get home that grass will be dry enough to get a good clipping," Mrs. Powell said. "Your papa can set under the apple tree and feast his eyes on a shipshape backyard."

Linda carried a pail of soapsuds and scrubbed the front porch. The beating rain had stirred up the summer dust and left streaks on the boards. After she'd rinsed away the winking soap bubbles, she stood at the corner of the house and looked down the street. No one was in sight except the man who came to look at the electric meters every month. She watched him go up on two porches and walk to the back of three houses. He skipped one place. *Probably 'cause they didn't pay what they owe and their lights are shut off again.*

Traffic sounds came from Eastside Avenue. Motors roared, tires squealed, and horns blared. Linda wondered how the people who lived over there could stand all the noise. But her mother pointed out that most of the houses had been made into stores. Carpets, stoves, secondhand furniture, and even fried chicken were sold in buildings which had been homes. Very few people actually lived along Eastside Avenue any longer.

When Linda walked into the kitchen her mother was sitting at the kitchen table counting money. "Feeling rich, Mama?"

"No, but I do feel a little free now that your papa's coming back for a steady spell. I was trying to figure if we could treat ourselves to hamburgers if there's a stand over where we're going."

"There is," Linda said. "Don't you remember, I told you. We stopped the day our class took a field trip to the dairy."

"Then we'll get ourselves ready and eat away from this kitchen for a change."

Linda sat with her mother on the bus, and the boys on the seat directly in front of them. "It's best to keep them in arm's reach," Mrs. Powell said. "In case they get a case of the giggles or the scuffles."

"I brought my money," Linda said. "You know,

the two dollars Grandma Powell sent for Christmas. Is that all right?"

"Good sakes, yes. It's yours. It slipped my mind that you were holding onto it all this time."

"Well, I had to make up my mind what I wanted most," Linda said. "The trouble is I kept changing. And I'm not real sure yet. Maybe I'll decide today."

They got off the Eastside bus at the downtown stop and waited on the slatted benches along the sidewalk. It was ten minutes before the mall bus chuffed to a stop. Freddie and Leo were sure they were going to die of thirst. But they stopped complaining when their mother promised they'd eat *before* they went shopping.

As they left the business district and headed south, Linda's mother said, "You didn't say what you were thinking of buying."

"Books, for one thing. But I guess maybe it's foolish with the library so near. Somehow, though, the look of books lined up on a shelf — my very own — makes me feel good — rich in a way."

"I don't know as there's anything wrong in that," her mother said. "If a couple of dollars' worth of books can make a lady feel rich, that'd be a good buy."

The bus stopped at a street corner to pick up three people. After the folding door clanged shut Mrs. Powell said, "I been noticing something about you, honey. Seems like you be a-talking different now that you're old enough to read a lot of books."

"What do you mean, Mama? How am I different?"

"I don't know as I can put it into words. But — yes I can. What you just said. 'How am I different!' I would've probably said, "How be I different?' "

Linda knew what her mother meant. She'd noticed that her own speech was changing. What she heard at school and the books she read were forming a new kind of pattern.

"I reckon you're getting educated," Mrs. Powell said.

"Does that make you feel bad, Mama? You sound a little sad."

"The truth is my feelings go two ways. I want my children to get a good education — better'n I had. But I don't want you to go off and leave me — grow away."

Linda slipped an arm through the crook of her mother's elbow and rubbed her face on her shoulder. "Mama, don't say such a thing. And I don't want you to leave me either. Not ever."

8

THE POWELLS, even the little boys, were too tired to talk much on the way home. They'd gotten off the bus at the Burger Chef, eaten, then crossed the four-lane highway to the shopping center. There was so much to see that they walked the whole length twice before deciding which stores had what they wanted to buy.

Freddie and Leo spent a lot of time at the pet store not because they expected to be able to take home a puppy, or even a parrakeet, but because they loved watching the animals. Mrs. Powell let Linda stay in the bookstore alone. It was nearly an hour before she made up her mind to spend her two dollars on a paperback she really wanted instead of three which were on sale.

The supermarket was the last stop. Mrs. Powell bought what was on her list, things like sugar and flour, catsup and tea bags. Then she subtracted their cost from the money she'd allotted for groceries. "We have nearly three dollars left for a real fine meal to welcome your papa. She chose his favorite foods — fresh pork sausage and sweet potatoes and was happy to find a bargain in fresh kale. "Some leaves be a little wilty," she said, "but a cold-water bath will snap them up."

The sun was slanting downward when they boarded the bus. Linda's mother put the brown bag of groceries on the floor and leaned back. "I'm purely tuckered out," she said. "All that walking. But it was worth it to see new things. Sometimes a body feels like she be walking in a tunnel that gets smaller all the time!"

She changed the subject and talked softly for a few minutes planning the meal of reunion. "I'll make squash pies. There's still a few cans of what I put up from last year's garden. Your papa do love squash pies."

"So do I, Mama," Linda said.

"Us too," Freddie added peeping over the back of the seat.

Nothing more was said until the bus rumbled across Eastside Avenue. "Your brothers be awful quiet," Mrs. Powell said. "Maybe they dozed off. You'd better see. We can't tote two boys when we already got these sacks to lug home from the corner."

The boys walked from the bus stop to the house, but their legs seemed stiff and they piled up on the couch as soon as Linda unlocked the door. "This house is stuffy," Mrs. Powell said. "Open up the windows — just the ones with screen wire. Fly time is here for sure."

Linda wanted to start reading her book. *But Mama will want me to put away groceries and help with supper. And I don't want to begin until I can finish three or four chapters. That way I can get to know the people and go on with the story in my mind.*

The Powells were eating sausage gravy on hot biscuits when Corey's mother came to the back door. "I'll snitch a little of tomorrow's meat and fry it into crumbles for flavor," Mrs. Powell had said.

The boys seemed to get a fresh start after they had eaten. They were running small trucks in the boxed-in sandpile when Corey's mother left.

Linda had washed the dishes and brushed up the supper crumbs by the time her mother came back into the kitchen. She was shaking her head and biting her lip.

"Something wrong, Mama?"

"Well, yes. And something's right too. Come in and sit a while." Linda forgot about being in a hurry to start her new book as she listened to her mother.

"Miss Williams be going back to Alabama — taking Corey with her," Mrs. Powell said.

"You think that's a bad thing? Is that why you shook your head?"

"No, just surprised. I mean I don't know Corey's mama too good. And what I thought I knew don't match up with what I heard."

She told Linda that Mrs. Williams had been thinking of going back to live with her mother for a long
time. "She knows there's not much chance to earn
money. But she knows, too, that it don't take much
to get by. It's 'cause of Corey she's making the
break."

" 'Cause Corey's been leaning toward Gloria's
group," Linda said.

"That's about the size of it."

"But couldn't Mrs. Williams say no? And stay home
more?"

"Not if she lives with her man!" Mrs. Powell said.
"He lays down the law, especially when he drinks. If
she don't listen, he don't give her no money to
spend on necessaries."

Linda didn't say anything for a while. She wondered
if Corey wanted to go to Alabama. Would things be
better or worse down there?

"What would you do, Mama, if you was in Corey's
mother's shoes?"

"What can I say to that?" Mrs. Powell said. "I'm
not feeling the same pinch, so I got no right to say
how I'd step. All I know, it must be a hard thing for
Corey's mama to decide. I guess last night made up
her mind!"

"You mean Corey being afraid and coming over
here?"

"Yes. She told me she already knowed it was wrong
to leave a girl Corey's age by herself. She'd told her
man that. But he paid no mind to what she said. So
they're leaving tomorrow. She borrowed enough
money from her brother."

"I thought that Corey's Uncle Biff didn't have any

money. That he just came here when he's out."

"Seems like we thought wrong. Could be he was around to look after his sister — and Corey."

Linda went out and sat on the back step. She wanted to talk to Corey but was afraid to go across the alley to her house. "Maybe they're going to slip away from Mr. Williams and I'd let the cat out of the bag by going to say good-bye."

The sun was almost down. A few streaks of gold ran through the gray sky. Linda hugged her knees and rocked back and forth singing parts of a song. The words had been running through her mind for an hour or more.

Shepherd, show me how to go
Over the hillside steep;
How to gather, how to sow,
How to feed Thy sheep.

She didn't know where she'd heard the tune. At church maybe? Or on the radio? Why did the words come to her mind now? *Is it because it seems like so many people need the Good Shepherd?*

"Singing to yourself?" a voice said from the side yard. Linda looked up and saw Corey coming toward her.

"I was wanting to talk to you."

I figured you would," Corey said. "My mama told me she'd talked to yours."

"Sit down," Linda said. "Or would you rather go in the house?"

"Here's good enough."

"How do you feel about going down to your grandma's?"

Corey's answer and the tone of her voice surprised

Linda. "I'm *glad* and excited. Mama couldn't believe the way I took the news. She doesn't know how many times I thought of running away — down to Gram's little house."

"Why, Corey? What makes moving seem great? Because here's not good?"

"Partly maybe," Corey said. "But not mostly. I've been to Willow Creek three or four times. Once for a whole week. I never did know a better place — for me anyways. Hills and flowers and pale blue smoke curling out of chimmeys. And my gram — well, she's probably never yelled at anyone in all her born days."

"Well," Linda said. "I'm relieved. I thought you'd be all torn up. Pulled between your parents and this school and the one down there maybe."

"Most of the time I never really felt like I had two parents," Corey said. "Just Mama and her not thinking about me much. Now I know she does. You know something? I feel more cared about than I have in my whole life."

That's both sad and good, Linda thought.

Neither girl spoke for a while. The air was cooler and Linda was thinking she'd better go in and get a sweater.

"I've got to go," Corey said. "Mama said for me to pack up my belongings while she's out buying what we need, like sneakers for me and a present for Gram."

"Do you think you'll ever come back?" Linda asked.

"I sure hope not," Corey said. "Mama the same as said it'd be up to me if I did or not. Of course, I'm not going to forget you, Linda. You've been a friend. Plenty of times."

74

"I'll write to you if you give me your address."

"I about forgot. It's here on this scrap of a grocery sack. And my mama says to tell yours she's sure obliged — for talking to her and giving her word she wouldn't blab to anyone."

Linda felt a little uncomfortable. She didn't like good-byes — not even when someone was going away for only a little while. *And this seems like a forever kind of parting. I don't think I'll ever ever see Corey.*

"Wait a minute," she said. "Stay right here. She hurried through the house and on upstairs. She rummaged through the top drawer of her dresser and found the red plastic headband Corey liked. She asked her mother's permission to give it away before going out on the back steps. "Here, Corey, this is to remember me by."

"I don't need anything for that. But it will be nice to look at it and know you wanted me to have it."

"Then take it, and don't just look at it. Wear it!" Linda said.

9

LINDA knew her father was home before she opened her eyes the next morning. She didn't hear his voice. It was the smell of coffee that led her to jump out of bed and hurry downstairs. *He has to be here. Mama always drinks tea,* she thought as she hurried through the living room.

Her parents were sitting at the table talking, and they didn't hear her barefoot steps. She stopped in the doorway and looked, taking in the joy of having her father home. The early morning sun glinted on his glasses. She couldn't see his dark eyes but she knew how they looked. She hoped hers had the same golden flecks. That's why she hadn't objected when the eye doctor said she should wear glasses for reading. Anything that was like her father was good.

Linda pretended to cough before she said, "Hey! I'm here."

Her father set his cup down so quickly that it danced on the saucer and walnut-brown liquid slurped over the sides. In two steps and one swoop he cradled Linda in his strong arms and whirled her around three times. He'd done this when he came home for as long as she could remember. Now she was so tall that her feet brushed against the door facing.

"Am I ever glad to see you," Joe Powell said. "You're about like I remembered you. Haven't changed to speak of."

"Papa, it's only been six weeks. But it seems longer."

"It sure does," her father said. "Time drags when you board in one room by your loneself."

"Want to eat now, Linda?" her mother asked. "The weather's a little cooler this morning, so I fixed oatmeal."

They talked about many things — the trouble at the Williams home, the trip to the mall, the small garden in the backyard. "That reminds me," Linda's mother said. "We need to get over to the corn and bean patch and get rid of some weeds."

"I'll take care of that," Mr. Powell said.

"You're not going to work today?" Linda asked.

"Not until midnight," her father said. "I'll be out with hoot owls for a while."

Linda knew what was ahead. Her father would sleep mornings and they'd all have to be quiet. This wasn't easy. *But at least Papa's here*, she thought. *That's*

He cradled Linda in his strong arms and twirled her around three times.

worth putting up with a little bad.

"If you be going to the garden, then you'll have company," Linda's mother said.

"Company," Mr. Powell said. "Helpers would be better."

"How about helping company, Papa?" Linda asked.

"We'll take along some sandwiches in case we don't get back by noon. I'll leave the sausage and squash pies till suppertime."

"You mean my mouth will have to water for a piece of pie till evening?" Linda's father asked.

"No. I reckon I could spare one to lug over to the garden," Linda's mother said. "As far as that goes, you could have a slice now. I don't know as anyone ever passed a law saying a body couldn't eat pie for breakfast."

"I've wondered about that lots of times," Linda said. "Who decided what should be eaten when?"

"Habit takes over," her father said.

"With some folks, yes," Mrs. Powell answered. "Others are just bothered by the habit of eating. Hunger makes anything right any old time. Maybe even oatmeal three times a day."

Within half an hour the five members of the Powell family crossed Eastside Avenue on the way to their vegetable garden. No buses ran to that edge of town and their car needed two new tires. The boys ran ahead. Freddie pulled the hoe behind him, the metal clanking as it bounced on the cracked sidewalk.

"Keep the sharp edge up," Mr. Powell called. "Or it'll be dull and nicked."

"Just you wait," Linda's mother said. "When we

be at the corn patch they won't be so full of zip."

By evening the whole family was ready to rest. They sat in the backyard from suppertime until the sun was down. The boys spread an old blanket on the grass, rolled up in it, and were soon drowsy.

"You oughta get you a few hours' sleep," Linda's mother said. " 'Fore you go on the night turn."

"I reckon so, but I been looking forward to sitting out here under this tree in the cool of the evening. So I aim to do it for a spell. Right now I don't know of a place I'd rather be than in this backyard."

"Well, this patch of ground's all right," Mrs. Powell said. "But I'd as soon as it was another street."

"Things take time, Roxanne. Things take time."

While it was still light enough to see, tires screeched and brakes squealed from somewhere near. Someone came running down the alley. It was the voices that told Linda that Gloria and Aggie were coming.

"Hurry it, Angelina. The guys won't wait forever."

"Maybe they'll have to," Aggie said. "I don't know as I want to go anyhow."

"You be stupid, really stupid. You saw that car."

That's all Linda heard before the girls disappeared.

"You'd think that girl's folks didn't have the price of a haircut," Linda's father said.

"That's the style, Papa," Linda said.

"I like yours better. Yours is neatly combed. Theirs — well, I can't think of a word for it.

"Everyone to their own taste, I always say," Linda's mother said. "But I'd surely hate to have to get the tangles out of Gloria's hair."

No one spoke for a few minutes. Then Linda's mother took a deep breath. "Summer's sure a-flyin' by. By the time sweet corn silks begin to show, like on ours, fall's only a little ways around the corner."

Linda leaned against the trunk of the lopsided apple tree and clasped her hands around her knees. Her mother's words made her feel a little sad. Fall meant school and for the first time in her life she dreaded for it to begin. The thought was like a sudden and icy shower. It swept over her all at once.

I don't understand myself, she thought. *School's always been one of the very best things. What's happening to me — to life?* She looked up through the umbrella of apple leaves and could see the glint of one trembling star. *Is it because Corey's gone. Am I feeling lonesome or left out? But that doesn't make much sense. I've never been best friends with Corey. And school's been great in spite of other kids, whether they were friendly or not.*

She shook her head, not wanting to look ahead to a time when a good thing might be spoiled. *Papa's home and has a job here. That's good. Anyway, a lot is better than it has been.*

For some reason after she was in bed Linda thought of Amory. She wondered if she'd see her again and how the tall girl with the long golden hair was feeling about her parents now. *Will she end up loving one and hating the other or being disappointed with both?*

She raised up on one elbow and turned her pillow over, thumping it twice with a doubled fist to make it fluffy. *Why do I keep myself awake thinking about other people's troubles? I never used to do that. Why do I now? Is this a part of growing up?*

Growing up must mean a lot of different things. Not the same to everyone.

10

AM I a misfit, Linda thought as she walked toward the library the next afternoon. She knew what the word meant and she'd heard it used many times. *But I never did think it had anything to do with me.*

She knew she didn't feel like she belonged in some places and with some people. *But that never bothered me. 'Cause I didn't want to be where I wasn't wanted or where I didn't want to be.*

She thought of the girls who'd been in the same class with her for five years. That was almost everyone. People in this direction from Eastside didn't move much. That took money and there weren't many better places for them to go. *They all think I'm a baby. And maybe I am. To them.*

A car pulled up in one of the slanted parking lanes at the side of the library as Linda came within sight of the cement block building. *That's Amory.*

The tall girl waited for Linda. "I hoped I'd see you," Amory said.

"Well, I been thinking about you too."

"That's nice. To be remembered is always good — if it's done with friendly thoughts."

"It is."

"Same here," Amory said. "But there's something else. A special reason why I wanted to see you. I'm your big sister."

"I don't understand what you mean," Linda said.

"Of course not," Amory said. "It's a new thing. Just got started this week — as far as I know. Mr. Wilson called us — there were about twenty of us, I think — all former Parkview students."

Linda was even more puzzled. She didn't know Mr. Wilson or that Amory had gone to Parkview Junior High School. "And what does that have to do with me? I won't be going to any junior high for another year."

"Come on in the library," Amory said. "I'll tell you as I work. Today's my turn to put books back in the stacks. That doesn't take too much concentration."

Before the two-tiered cart was unloaded Linda learned that she *was* to go to Parkview Junior High, not when she was a seventh-grader but the coming fall. Amory said that Parkview was being made into a middle school which included sixth-graders. "There's been a lot of shifting around, only they call it redistricting. You mean you never read about it in the newspaper?"

"We don't take the paper," Linda said.

"Even so," Amory said. "It looks like you'd have been told. Of course, it could be a sudden thing. Let's scoot this cart down to the biography section."

"I don't even know for sure where Parkview is," Linda said.

"It's north of here, sort of on the edge of town. The building's fairly new, five years old, or maybe six."

Linda was excited over the idea of going to a new school, but there were questions in her mind. "How far away is this building? Will I have to walk. How much would bus fare be?"

"You'll hear all about it at the meeting," Amory said. "I'll come get you — be your own special school bus driver."

"What meeting? When?"

"Oh, I didn't tell you. Well, it'll be a couple of weeks from now. Letters are being sent to all sixth-graders at your school. Invitations really. You're to be at Parkview all day. Take a tour. Eat lunch there. And people like me, who've been there, will be guides. You'll also meet the sixth-graders from that district who are being transferred."

Linda wondered. *Will nearly everyone over there be white?* This wouldn't make any difference to her. *But it might to them.*

"How do you feel about the change?" Amory asked as they pushed the empty cart back to the charge desk.

"For myself it sounds great," Linda said. "This summer I haven't been looking forward to school as much as usual." She didn't explain the reason. "But I don't think everyone will go over to the meeting!"

"Why?" Amory asked. "Do you think they will be against moving?"

"Some will. Change scares a lot of people. But that wasn't what I meant. Not everyone will read those letters. Any kind of note from school scares them. Like they're sure their kids are in trouble."

"I wonder if the people in the administration office know this?" Amory asked.

"Probably," Linda said. "I imagine they've run into such problems before."

As Linda walked home she wished she could see the school which would be new to her. *Amory never really said how far away it is. And even if I could walk over there Mama might not let me go alone.*

She didn't say anything about the transfer until they were eating supper. The evening meal was later than usual, now that her father was sleeping in the daytime. "If I don't set it up this way us Powells won't be sitting at the table at the same time all summer. 'Cepting on Sundays," Linda's mother said.

Linda was trying to show Freddie how to wind spaghetti around his fork. "I 'bout forgot," Roxanne Powell said. "We got a letter from school today. I can't be making heads or tails of it."

"Let me see it," Linda's father said.

"I know what it says," Linda said.

She explained what she'd heard from Amory.

"I wonder why they be doing all this moving around?" Linda's mother said. "Like kids are checkers on a board. How we get Linda way over there?"

"There'll be a way," Joseph Powell said.

"But what's the need?" Mrs. Powell asked.

"That's why I want to read the letter," Linda's father said. He polished his glasses, then read, and reread. "This explains things," he said. "They've shut up two old grade schools, making the others crowded. So they're putting sixth-graders in junior highs and giving them a new name."

"Middle schools," Linda said.

"That's right," her father said. "How do you feel about this, Linda?"

"Okay, I guess," Linda said. "But I can't be sure until I know more."

"There'll be a plenty of complaining," Linda's mother said. "Folks don't take easy to change. 'Less it's the kind they take in their very own hands."

Linda left the table and followed her brothers out to the backyard. The little boys were running small trucks over roads they'd made in their sand pile. They made humming noises for motors and beeping sounds of horns. The moon was high in the sky. "Only it's just half a moon, like a thin slice of pale gold orange."

She sat down on the back step and hugged her doubled-up knees. Loud music came from across the alley. *Probably it's Gloria's. Her record player's got a lot of volume. She must be home for a change. Probably got company.*

Linda let thoughts of Gloria flit out of her mind. She had plenty of other things to think about. For the first time since Amory told her that Eastside sixth-graders would be going to Parkview, Linda tried to visualize how the new school would be. *I can't really picture it. How can I when I've never seen the building? And I don't know anyone over there — not that I know of.*

All at once, and this was strange, Linda felt as if she'd already left the old school. It was like she was about to have an adventure, a new experience in her mind. She was ready for whatever was ahead. This was a good feeling and it lasted until she was nearly asleep. Then Amory's words came to her mind.

The two girls had parted in the parking lot. "In case I don't see you before, I'll pick you up at eight on the day of the visit to Parkview."

"Do you know where I live?"

"About. Mrs. Ferguson told me."

As Linda remembered she propped herself up on one elbow. *Why didn't I tell Amory I'd meet her at the library? So she wouldn't have to go out of her way.*

Then Linda burrowed her head in her pillow and shut her eyes. *That's not true and I know it. It's only four blocks. I'm just afraid Amory won't like me anymore if she sees where I live.*

11

THE WEATHER changed during the night. Linda was shivering when she awoke. She reached for a blanket without opening her eyes. She was soon warm enough to go back to sleep but lay listening to the sounds. Rain was splattering against the windowpane and wind was rumbling the tin roof.

The skies were gray all day and the rain didn't end until evening. It was difficult for Linda and her brothers to be quiet so that their father could sleep. *I could keep still myself,* she thought, *but not when I have to entertain the boys. It takes so much talking — or whispering.*

After lunch she thought of an idea of making a hideout on the front porch. She took two old blankets and spread them over the porch swing, fastening them together with clothespins. "Boy, oh boy," Freddie said. "A double-decker hideout."

Linda sat in the rocking chair with the broken arm and read and sometimes daydreamed. Her long-sleeved sweat shirt kept out the damp chill of the day. And the rain came from the south and didn't hit the porch.

Very few people walked past the house and none looked her way. They kept their heads turned against the driving shower. Linda finished the book she'd bought at the shopping center — for the second time. She felt as if the people were real, and rereading was like a visit with friends. This was the way her favorite books always made her feel. *And these friends won't ever get mad at me or think they're too grown up to run around with me.*

She started rocking and pushing herself into motion with one foot. The squeaking of the chair kept her from hearing footsteps. She didn't know anyone had come up the walk until Aggie said, "You're liable to get wet out here.

Linda was startled and especially surprised to see Aggie. *She hasn't been in our yard for a long time — at least not as far as I know.* "How about yourself?" she said aloud. "Your hair has raindrops all over."

"Maybe," Aggie said. "But none's down to the skin yet. I've not been out long. Just the time it takes to cross the alley and come around your house."

Linda got up. "Here take the chair. I'll sit on the

96

stool. I'd ask you in, but Papa's not awake. He works nights and sleeps days."

"So does mine . . . sleep days, I mean. Nights, he mostly drinks . . . at the Zebra, I guess."

Linda couldn't think of anything to say to Aggie. For one thing they hadn't really talked for a long time and it was like they had to get acquainted. *And besides I can't help wondering why she's here.*

Freddie raised the blanket and looked out. "I thought someone was talking," he said. "Besides us."

"You haven't said much yourself for a while," Linda said.

"That's cause Leo's asleep," Freddie said. "Stretched out in the swing seat."

"Then what have you been doing?"

"Oh! Running my car. Playing like the boards are race tracks."

Linda's mother came to the door with three large molasses cookies. "Oh, I didn't know we has company," she said. "I'll get an extra."

"You don't need to," Linda said. "Leo's sound asleep."

"This cookie's warm like it's just been baked," Aggie said.

"It has. That's what Mama's doing."

"Mine don't bake a thing. She goes to the day-old bread store and gets broken stuff." Aggie took little bites and didn't say anything for a while. "You heard about this middle school business?"

"Yes."

"You think it's okay?"

"Well, I don't know that it won't be," Linda said. "And I guess we'll have to wait and see."

"I s'pose," Aggie said. "At first I thought it was a clunky idea — going all that way. Then somebody came up with the notion that there'd be new boys over that way. Older ones too."

Linda almost said, "I'll bet Gloria thought of that."

"That don't make no difference to you, does it?" Aggie asked. Her brown eyes looked right into Linda's, like the answer was real important.

Linda shrugged. "I hadn't thought about that part of changing schools. I guess I'm not in any hurry to grow up."

"Sometimes I wish I hadn't been," Aggie said. "But it's too late. A body can't go back. Seems like you can't anyhow."

An old car came down the street, its plum paint glistening in the rain. Tires whined on the wet pavement. "I gotta go," Aggie said. "Be across the alley and home before that car stops. In case my pa's awake."

Aggie seems so sad, Linda thought. *As if she doesn't like herself very well. I hope I never let myself get that way. But how does it happen?*

The Powells had meant to work in the garden that evening, but the rain kept them at home. "Why can't we go anyhow?" Freddie asked. "I like walking in the rain."

"I know," his father said. "Sometimes I think you are first cousin to a duck. But the ground will be wet. Working it now would pack it as hard as cement."

Linda thought of the little rain tree in the backyard. Her father had shown her how to loosen the soil around the slender trunk. "Got to give a plant room to breathe," he said. "So it won't be stunted."

But it still hasn't bloomed, Linda thought as she slid plates into soapy suds. *Could it be I didn't take good enough care of it?* 'Cause *Mama keeps telling me everything has its own blossoming time and the sprays of leaves are bright green.*

The Powells walked across and up the street to visit Mrs. Mozely. Linda's mother took a half-dozen molasses cookies and three peony buds. "Why didn't you pick the opened-out flowers, Mama?" Linda asked. "The pink ones are so pretty."

"I know," her mother said. "But buds be better for Mrs. Mozely. She can watch them unfold. Give her a reason for looking forward."

The lonely neighbor was so glad to have visitors. She fluttered around finding chairs for everyone and dug a small bag of peppermints from the corner of the drawer. Linda wished she'd tell or retell stories of her life in the South. But the conversation didn't follow the long-ago path. Instead the grown-ups talked mostly about the problems of people on this side of the avenue.

"Seems like times don't get any better," Mrs. Mozely said.

"Do you think they're worse?" Mr. Powell asked.

"No. I can't say that I do. Seems like things stay the same. As far as I can see, them that tries balances the scales against the givers-up. Maybe that's as much as we can hope for. Not to be outweighed."

"I can't agree," Linda's father said. "When *I* give up hoping for betterment I might join the not-trying side."

"You know better than that, Joseph Powell," Mrs.

Mozely said. "I knowed your pa and ma before you and watched you all your life. You'll keep on trying."

"And hoping," Linda's father said. "Now! We'd better amble back. It's time to get these children to bed and me off to the wire mill."

The air was cool and clean. The rain was over. Linda saw one star in the eastern sky. She hugged her father's arm as they crossed the street. She felt safe, deep down safe. She thought of Aggie and wondered if she sometimes had this feeling. *Does she ever? Or has she lost it somewhere?*

12

LINDA didn't see Amory at the library until two days before time to get acquainted with Parkview school. In the two weeks Linda's feelings about being transferred went up and down like the bumping teeter-totter in the park. Sometimes she felt excited and looked forward to meeting new kids and having different teachers. Other times she dreaded change. *I know how it is over here. The new school might be better, but it could be worse.*

The Powell family went to their garden patch at the edge of town before Linda went to the library. "The wet ground has kept us out and given the weeds a head start," Joseph Powell said. "We best try to get ahead of them 'fore I take time to sleep."

They came home at noon weary, hungry, and hot. "This be a day for a quick cold meal," Linda's mother said, as she took lunch meat from the refrigerator and opened a can of pork and beans. Linda measured water into the brown stone pitcher and added a package of lemonade mix. Her brothers took their plates to the backyard and their father went to bed as soon as he ate.

"What you going to do, Mama?" Linda asked.

"For a little bit I am going to rest — do nothing at all. Then I'll tackle Mrs. Ramsey's ruffled curtains. They sure am pretty — until it comes to ironing."

"Is it okay if I wear my new skirt to the library?" Linda asked. "If I promise to be careful."

"Why you wanting to dress up to go over there? You thinking you'll run onto some boy?"

"Oh, Mama. I never once thought of such a thing. Besides, I wouldn't know of anyone I'd dress up for."

"You will. Give you time."

"I just want to wear the skirt because it's new — and swirly, with all the pleats."

"Well, I guess there aren't no harm in you feeling good about being dressed up — even if it's not Sunday."

Linda's father had bought each of the family something they'd especially wanted with his first paycheck. The boys, after debating a long time, chose whiffle balls and plastic bats. Their mother had wanted pink geraniums for her kitchen window for three summers. And Linda was delighted when they found the peacock blue skirt with accordion pleats on the sale table.

At first Linda didn't recognize Amory. "You have a
new hairdo," she said.

The flaw in the fabric didn't show after her mother's mending. It was mostly hidden in the fold.

The lacy white top her grandmother had crocheted and sent in the Christmas box went just right with the skirt. Linda was glad now that her mother hadn't allowed her to wear it every time she'd asked. It was as good as new.

I don't really know why I'm going to the library, Linda thought as she crossed the street. *I still have one book of the stack I took out last week. Maybe I want to check and see if there are any new ones. And besides going's always a good thing for me.*

She'd wondered several times how old a person had to be to become a library aide. She knew Amory was sixteen. *Are there any younger? Four years is a long time to wait.*

Amory was at the desk. At first Linda didn't recognize her. "You have a new hairdo."

"I suddenly got tired of letting it hang," Amory said. "In hot weather it feels better to wear it up. Like it?"

"Yes, I do. It sort of frames your face. And it's — lovely."

"Thank you," Amory said. "And I can say the same for you — and mean it too."

Linda stayed in the cool shaded room for over an hour. Part of the time she and Amory talked about the visit to the middle school.

"I know a lot more about it than when I first told you," Amory said. "All the big sisters and brothers — most of them anyway — had a meeting Thursday night. There'll be a sack lunch at noon, provided by the school cafeteria, and small groups will meet for an hour. They'll be made up of a mixture of people from the three elementary schools who are transferring. This is to help you get acquainted."

Linda wondered, *Which schools does she mean? From what part of town?* But she didn't ask.

Amory wrote Linda's address on a file card and said, "Remember, I'll pick you up."

Linda changed her clothes as soon as she got home. She wanted the new outfit to look nice for the trip to the new school. The change seemed real to her now, not just something that might happen. She thought about Gloria and Aggie and the other girls. *Do they have big sisters? Probably so. Would they like being split up and put in other groups? Probably not.*

Linda was ready half an hour before Amory came. She sat on the porch a few minutes, then wandered around to the backyard. She didn't want to sit down out there, because the bench and chairs were still wet with early morning dew. She walked over to the rain tree and ran a finger over a leaf's lacy edge. She saw something that could be buds along a stem. Was it finally getting ready to bloom?

"Linda, honey," her mother called from the back door. "Someone to see you."

Amory came out the door and said, "You ready?"

"Yes, I've been watching for you — until I came out here. I didn't mean for you to have to get out."

"That's okay," Amory said. "We have plenty of time. And this way I got to meet your mother. I'll be careful, Mrs. Powell."

The rest of the day was a little like a ride on a merry-go-round. Linda met so many people, saw so many new sights, and heard so many new ideas that she couldn't focus on any one of them. She'd have to do that later, in her mind, and when she told her mother and father what she'd seen and heard.

Almost everyone Linda met was friendly. Amory had a lot to do with making Linda feel comfortable and with helping her meet others. All sixth-grade teachers were in their rooms and took time to talk with anyone who was not too shy to approach them.

By the time Amory backed her car out of the Parkview lot Linda felt as if she was already at home in the new school. *Maybe everything over here won't be so great. But I'm not scared now.*

She tried to tell Amory how much she appreciated her kindness. "I don't know why you're so good to me," she said. "But it's nice."

"You don't know? You really don't, do you? You can't see how special you are, can you?"

"No. I'm just — well, whatever I am."

"I have to say this," Amory said as they waited for a stoplight to change from red to green. "You've really helped me. I mean, since I met you, I've realized that an awful lot of people make too much fuss over differences that don't exist."

Linda didn't know what to say. She understood what Amory meant, but what was there to say?

"Have I made you uncomfortable?" Amory asked as she reached over and touched Linda's hand.

"No. I was just thinking. I could say the same thing you did. About how much we're alike. I guess there are a lot of ways people are different."

"There certainly are," Amory said as she turned and headed toward the other end of Eastside Avenue.

"In the way people think and act mostly."

The girls changed the subject and talked about the coming of school again. "This is my last year," Amory said. "In a way I'm glad. I'll probably go to college. Somewhere away from this town. I used to think I'd go to the university here, so I could be at home and keep working at the library. But things are different now."

It was four o'clock when they pulled up in front of the Powell house. Linda heard the four toots of the factory whistle. "I'll not see you for a while," Amory said. "I'm going to stay with my father for a month in Virginia. But I'll be back at my job here during August."

"I'll miss you," Linda said.

"You're sweet." Amory reached over and cupped Linda's face in her hands. "Don't ever change, Linda Powell. And I wish I could keep people from hurting you."

13

THE SUN woke Linda the next morning. *It must be late*, she thought. *It's never in my eyes when I open them.* She locked her arms behind her head and thought about the people she'd met at Parkview. *It's like the world is suddenly wider. Now I want school to begin. And I'm glad about that!*

She heard no sounds from the other rooms in the house. *Papa's probably asleep and Mama's shooed the boys outside!* She heard the clank of the mailbox lid as she crossed the living room. She waited until the postman clumped across the porch before opening the screen door and reaching for the mail. The air smelled like flowers. *What's in bloom?* She stepped out and saw starlike flowers on the mock orange bush at the southwest corner. She took a deep breath, loving the fragrance.

Then she looked at the mail, two letters and an advertisement listing the items on sale at the supermarket. One letter was from her grandmother, Linda knew without reading. No one else wrote to them in spider-web handwriting. The other letter was addressed to Linda. She tore it open and turned the bluelined page over to see the signature. "Your friend, Corey Druscilla Williams."

Linda hurried through the house and out to the backyard. Her mother was sitting under the spreading limbs of the lopsided apple tree. She was sewing a patch on a pair of faded blue jeans. The needle glinted in the sun as she carefully wove the thread into a briar stitch.

"Here's a letter from Grandma," Linda said.

"Well, thank goodness. I been wondering if they'd run out of paper down there."

"I got one too," Linda said. "From Corey."

Linda sat down on the grass and read and then reread the letter. Corey said she was having a great time and that her mother had found a job working at a laundry five miles away. "She catches a bus down in the valley and the pay's enough to keep us real well."

"What does Corey have to say for herself?" Linda's mother asked.

"Well, she sounds happy. Says there's a new family halfway up the hill from her grandma's. With girls near her age. Anything new with *my* grandma?"

"No. Not to speak of. She wants us to come down for a spell. But that's not new."

"You think we'll go?"

"I can't see ahead to say for sure. We got to catch up 'fore we buy new tires. A body can't keep spending and get caught up at the same time. You hankering to go South? Like usual?"

Linda thought a while before she answered. "Oh, I'd like to go. But it doesn't seem as important as it did even last year. I wonder why that is."

"It be natural," her mother said. "A part of growing up, of flying on your own wings. Doing family things don't always come first. Every single body goes through this, I reckon."

"But I'd want to go. Not be left behind," Linda said.

"No one of us would be in favor of *that*," her mother said.

"Where are the boys?" Linda asked.

"They went hiking with that teacher, Mr. Haines. He came by and asked just them. Said he needed company."

"Where were they going?"

"Out to where the new road is being built. The boys will more'n likely be making noises like bulldozers and such machinery when they play in that sand pile."

Aggie and Gloria came down the alley on the way to Eastside Avenue. They didn't look toward the Powell yard.

"Did they go over to that new school?" Mrs. Powell asked.

"Yes. I saw them once in the morning," Linda

said. "But not after that."

"They likely as not skipped out with boys."

"Maybe," Linda said. "I didn't want to leave, to miss anything."

"You kind of excited about this move?"

"Yes, I am, Mama. At first I wasn't, but now — well, I wouldn't care if school began tomorrow or even today."

"I guess that's another thing that can't be hurried," her mother said. "By the way, are you hungry?"

"Yes, I am. But I'll fix my own breakfast. You sit still. After I eat I think I'll answer Corey's letter. There's so much to tell her."

She wrote a six-page letter, using three sheets of notebook paper, filling both sides. The noon whistle at the factory blew as she addressed the envelope. *If I hurry maybe I can get this to the corner mailbox before the pickup truck comes.*

Her mother asked her to go to the market for sweet rolls and dried beef. "I'll stir up some baking-powder biscuits and make the gravy when you get back. Why don't you stop and see if Mrs. Mozely be needing someone to run an errand?"

Linda's father was downstairs by the time she delivered the neighbor's pint of strawberry ice cream and five pounds of potatoes.

"I think I'll mosey over to the garden," Mr. Powell said as they ate. "The peas could be filled out. Enough for a mess anyway. And there's likely to be radishes."

"Want us to go along?"

"Not 'less you're hankering to take a walk. This job don't take two, let alone three."

116

Linda's mother said someone should be around when the boys came back. "And I was figuring on hemming that school dress I been working on," she added.

"Go ahead," Mr. Powell said. "I'll be back shortly."

After the hem was measured and pinned, Linda's mother took her sewing to the circle of shade under the apple tree. Linda spread a blanket on the grass and read for a long time. The sounds of the traffic on Eastside Avenue seemed to fade away. She was living the story on the pages. When she came to the end, she shut her eyes and tried to imagine what would happen to the twins who hated the idea of moving to the small town. Would they make the best of things? Find new friends? Or go on pouting? That's the way she always felt about favorite books. She wanted the people to go on living in her mind.

She rested her head on her doubled-up arm and looked up through the leaves of the tree. She could see glints of sunlights and splotches of blue sky. She shifted her eyes to the little rain tree. *Can it be?* she thought. She jumped up and ran across the walk. "Look, Mama! It's blooming. See the sprays of yellow flowers!"

"I know," her mother said. "I saw them as soon as I walked out the door."

"Why didn't you tell me? You know how I've worried and been afraid it would never have any flowers."

"Yes I did. But I knowed it'd be more fun if you saw it for yourself."

"There are going to be more blossoms," Linda said excitedly. "I see little buds. I'd begun to think

117

my little tree was different. That it'd never bloom."

"Everything does, honey," her mother said. "In its own time, and its own way — when things are as they should be."

DOROTHY HAMILTON was born in Delaware County, Indiana, where she still lives. She received her elementary and secondary education in the schools of Cowan and Muncie, Indiana. She attended Ball State University, Muncie, and has taken work by correspondence from Indiana University, Bloomington, Indiana. She has attended professional writing courses, first as a student and later as an instructor.

Mrs. Hamilton grew up in the Methodist Church and participated in numerous school, community, and church activities until the youngest of her seven children was married.

Then she felt led to become a private tutor. This service has become a mission of love. Several hundred girls and boys have come to Mrs. Hamilton for gentle encouragement, for renewal of self-esteem, and to learn to work.

The experiences of motherhood and tutoring have inspired Mrs. Hamilton in much of her writing.

Seven of her short stories have appeared in quarterlies and one was nominated for the American Literary Anthology. Since 1967 she has had fifty serials published, more than four dozen short stories, and several articles in religious magazines. She has also written for radio and newspapers.

Mrs. Hamilton is author of *Anita's Choice, Christmas for Holly, Charco, The Killdeer, Tony Savala, Jim Musco, Settled Furrows, Kerry, The Blue Caboose, Mindy, The Quail, Jason, The Gift of a Home, The Eagle, Cricket, Neva's Patchwork Pillow, The Castle,* and *Linda's Rain Tree.*